In the LAND of the MUSIC MACHINE™

Stories by Ane Weber

Illustrations by Mark Pendergrass

AGAPELAND® SERIES

 Chariot Books

THIS I LOVE TO READ BOOK . . .
- has been carefully written to be fun and interesting for the young reader.
- repeats words over and over again to help the child read easily and to build the child's vocabulary.
- uses the lyrical rhythm and simple style that appeals to children.
- is told in the easy vocabulary of the validated word lists for grades one, two, and three from the *Ginn Word Book for Teachers: A Basic Lexicon.*
- is written to a mid-second grade reading level on the Fry Readability Test.

Chariot Books is an imprint of David C. Cook Publishing Co.

David C. Cook Publishing Co., Elgin, Illinois 60120
David C. Cook Publishing Co., Weston, Ontario

IN THE LAND OF THE MUSIC MACHINE
© 1983 by Agape Force

First printing, 1984
Printed in the United States of America
89 88 87 86 85 84   5 4 3 2 1

Library of Congress Cataloging in Publication Data

Weber, Ane.
  In the land of the music machine.

  Summary: Animals and things in nature demonstrate ways to be good and kind.
  [1. Conduct of life—Fiction] I. Pendergrass, Mark D., ill. II. Title.
PZ7.W3874In 1984   [E]   83-21055
ISBN 0-89191-784-5 (pbk.)
ISBN 0-89191-835-3 (hc.)

Contents

5
A Land Called Love

13
Songs of the Music Machine

21
Herbert the Snail

29
The Kindness Club

35
Follow-the-Leader

41
Always Chasing Rainbows

47
Self-Control Day

55
The Little Breeze

62
Campfire

Stevie and Nancy rolled down a strange hill

in Wiley Woods.

They rolled faster and faster.

The blue sky,

the green grass,

the white clouds

melted together.

When they came to a stop,

everything was different.

Stevie saw tall, tall trees.

Taller than any he had ever seen.

Nancy saw big, big flowers.

Bigger than any she had ever seen.

"Where are we?" Nancy asked.

"I have never seen a place like this before."

"You are in Agapeland,"
said a voice behind them.
Stevie and Nancy turned around.
They saw a man in a long red coat.
His shiny buttons were shaped like hearts.
He stood by a big machine.

"I am the conductor in Agapeland,"

he said.

"Agapeland?" Stevie asked.

"Yes," said Mr. Conductor.

"Agapeland is the land of love."

Suddenly strange sounds came from

the big machine.

Whir, whir, chuka, chuka,

Bomp, bomp, psst.

"What is that?" Stevie asked.

"Our Music Machine,"

said Mr. Conductor.

"Your Music Machine?"

Stevie and Nancy said together.

"How does it work?"

"You put something in,"

said Mr. Conductor.

"And a song will come out."

He pulled one of the heart buttons

off of his coat.

Clang!

8 He dropped it into the machine.

The Music Machine began to bubble.

It began to shake.

Whir, whir, chuka, chuka,

bomp, bomp, psst!

Stevie and Nancy did not know

what would happen next.

The Music Machine became still.

It began to sing.

"Love is gentle.

Love is kind,

Love is leaving self behind."

"Love is patient.

Love is strong.

Love is righting every wrong."

The Music Machine stopped singing.

It ended with a

whir, whir, chuka, chuka,

bomp, bomp, psssssst!

"The Music Machine is wonderful!

This place is wonderful!"

Nancy said.

"I would like to live in this land of love,"

Stevie said. "How long can we stay?"

"As long as it takes

for you to learn about love,"

said Mr. Conductor.

"Just follow me.

We have lots to show you."

The next day Stevie and Nancy
went to see the Music Machine.
"Can we play it?"
they asked Mr. Conductor.
"Do you have something to put in?"
said Mr. Conductor.

Stevie dug into his pockets.
"No," he said sadly.
"How about a smile?" Mr. Conductor
asked.
"Just look into the slot on the side
of the machine.

Then smile a big smile."

"All right," said Stevie and Nancy.

They smiled into the slot on one side.

Whir, whir, chuka, chuka,

Bomp, bomp, psst.

The machine began to rattle and shake.

Then a beautiful tune began to play.

"What a happy song," said Nancy.

"But there aren't any words."

"That's because you make up the words,"

said Mr. Conductor.

"It's a song of joy."

"But I can't think of any words," said Stevie.

"You will," answered Mr. Conductor.

"You have to be full of joy
to make up the words."

Whir, whir, chuka, chuka,

Bomp, bomp, pssssst.

The Music Machine bumped and jumped.

It jumped and bumped.

Then bubbles began to fly

up the glass tube.

The music played faster and faster.

The bubbles danced higher and higher.

Bubbles of red and green.

16 Purple and pink.

Boom!

The glass tube flew off the machine.

All the bubbles came out the top.

Stevie stuck out his tongue.

A red bubble landed on it.

Pop!

"Cherry!" said Stevie.

"That bubble tasted like cherry!"

He caught a purple bubble,

and gave it to Nancy.

Pop!

"Grape!" said Nancy.

"That bubble tasted like grape!

All of the bubbles are flavored!"

"Watch this," said Stevie.

He opened his mouth.

He caught three bubbles at once!

"Yummmmmmm! What fun!"
Now he felt like singing.

And he knew the words to sing.

"See," Mr. Conductor said,

"you did think of words for the joy song.

As long as you are having fun,

any words are the right words."

Herbert the snail lived under a rock

in Agapeland.

His favorite place was the garden path,

because it was always so busy.

Ant walked up and down,

up and down,

carrying food to his anthill.

Spider spun in and out,

in and out,

making her lovely webs.

But Herbert did not like one thing.

"Everyone moves too slowly

on the path," he told his friends.

"I want to go fast.

Will you go fast, too?" he asked them.

"Not me," said Ant. "If I go fast,

I will drop my food.

I will have nothing to eat."

"Not me," said Spider.

"If I go fast,

I will spin a crooked web.

Then I will not be able

to catch my dinner."

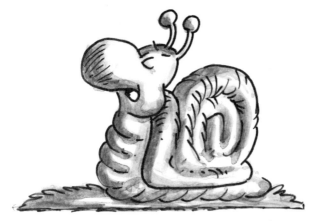

"Not me," said Cricket. "If I go fast,
I will easily be seen by a hungry bird.
I will become his dinner."

"Then I will go fast by myself,"
said Herbert.
He began to race up and down,
up and down,
up and down.
"Beep, beep, beep," he said
to everyone in his way.

One day Cricket was standing

in the path.

Cricket heard, "Beep, beep, beep."

He knew Herbert was coming.

But he could not get out of the way

in time.

"Oh, no!" he cried.

Crash! Bang! Boom!

Herbert ran into Cricket.

They both went flying through

Spider's beautiful new web.

Spider was mad.

Her web was ruined.

Cricket was mad.

His side hurt.

Ant was mad.

24 He had been watching.

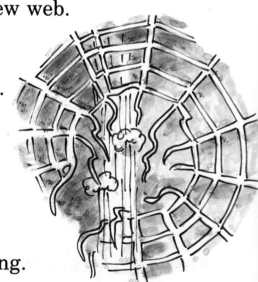

He knew Herbert was wrong

to go so fast.

No one would talk to Herbert.

Herbert was sad.

He went home.

He told his father what had happened.

"Have patience, Herbert," said his father.

"We all make mistakes,

if we go too fast.

But everything turns out right

when you are patient."

Herbert went back to the garden.

He told Cricket he was sorry.

He told Spider he was sorry.

He told Ant he was sorry.

He promised to slow down

to a proper snail's pace.

Now, if anyone is in too big a hurry,

Herbert smiles and says,

"Have patience. Have patience.

Remember, God is patient with us.

We must be patient, too."

Mr. Squirrel walked out of his hole.

He walked onto the limb of his tree.

"Oh, no!" he cried.

All the nuts he had stored for winter

were on the ground below him.

They had spilled out of his hole.

He went to get help.

When he returned,

the nuts were back in his hole.

"Who did this?" Mr. Squirrel asked.

But no one knew.

Then he saw a note on the ground.

It read,

"Today is your special day.   29

THE KINDNESS CLUB."

Mrs. Sparrow was building a nest

for her little sparrows.

She flew away to get more twigs.

When she returned,

the nest was finished.

"Who did this?" she asked.

But no one knew.

Then she saw a note in her nest.

It read,

"Today is your special day.

THE KINDNESS CLUB."

"Who is The Kindness Club?"

Mr. Squirrel asked Mrs. Sparrow.

"I know who they are,"

said Robin.

"If you are very quiet,

I will lead you to them."

Robin led Mr. Squirrel and Mrs. Sparrow

to the edge of the forest.

They saw Stevie and Nancy

by Brother Fox's hole.

The children put flowers on his door.

They placed a note in the flowers.

The birds knew it read,

"Today is your special day.

THE KINDNESS CLUB."

Mr. Squirrel and Mrs. Sparrow

ran up to Stevie and Nancy.

"Thank you," they cried.

"But tell us.

Why did you sign your note: the

Kindness Club?"

"Because kindness is treating others

32 the way you would like to be treated,"

Stevie explained.

"It's more fun,

if it's a surprise."

"We'd like to join the club, too,"

said Mr. Squirrel.

"If we help,

today can be a special day for all the

animals!"

One day Mr. Conductor and Nancy

took a walk through the green pasture.

Lamb skipped up to them.

"I'd like to play with you, Nancy,"

he said.

Nancy hugged Lamb's fluffy neck.

"You two may play here

while I go to the next pasture,"

said Mr. Conductor.

"Just be sure to stay away

from the stream over there."

"Don't worry about us,"

Nancy and Lamb said together.

They ran off through
the tall grass.

"I know a fun game," said Lamb.

"Let's play follow-the-leader."

"OK," said Nancy. "You start."

Lamb hopped.

Nancy hopped.

Lamb hopped and skipped.

Nancy hopped and skipped.

Lamb hopped and skipped and jumped.

Nancy hopped and skipped and jumped.

The game went on and on.

"I'm thirsty," said Nancy.

"But Mr. Conductor said to

stay away from the stream."

She looked at the water in the stream.

"If he knew how thirsty we are,

he would say a little drink is OK,"

said Lamb. "Follow me."

Nancy followed Lamb to the edge

of the stream.

She held onto Lamb's neck.

She leaned over the rushing water.

She leaned way out.

Splash!

Nancy fell into the icy water.

"Help!" shouted Nancy.

She clung to a small branch
at the edge of the stream.

"I can't reach you," cried Lamb.

"The water is too swift!"

"I will drown," shouted Nancy.

"The water is too deep!"

Just then, two large hands lifted
Nancy from the stream.

Mr. Conductor hugged Nancy close to
him.

"Thank you, Mr. Conductor," Nancy
cried.

"You saved my life."

"Do you remember what I said?"

Mr. Conductor asked.

"You said to be good,"

Nancy said.

"Goodness means obeying,"

Mr. Conductor said.

Lamb hung his head.

Nancy looked down at the ground.

"We're sorry we didn't obey,"

they said together.

"I forgive you,"

said Mr. Conductor.

"Just remember,

it's not always good

to follow the leader."

Stevie and Nancy sat on a hill.

They sang, "Rain, rain, go away.

Come again another day."

All of a sudden

the rain stopped.

The sun peeked out from

behind the clouds.

A red and yellow,

green and blue,

orange and pink

rainbow spread across the sky.

"The rainbow starts in the grass

over there!" said Stevie.

He pointed to some trees in front

of them.

"I wonder what would happen
if we stepped inside the rainbow,"
said Nancy.

"Do you think we would turn
all those colors?"

"Let's find out," said Stevie.

The children ran toward the rainbow.

They ran faster and faster.

But guess what?

The rainbow kept moving away

from them.

"Run even faster!" Stevie shouted.

They ran faster and faster.

Still the rainbow moved

farther and farther away.

"I'm tired," Nancy said.

"I want to stop running."

She sat down on the ground.

"Not me," Stevie shouted.

"Be careful!" Nancy cried.

"The grass is wet."

But it was too late.

Stevie slipped on the grass.

He began to tumble.

He tumbled down and down.

He tumbled down to the bottom

of the grassy hill.

When he looked up,

Mr. Conductor was there.

"We were trying to touch the rainbow,"

Stevie said.

"But we couldn't do it.

Maybe the rainbow isn't real."

"The rainbow is real, all right,"

said Mr. Conductor.

"But you need to have faith."

"Faith?" asked Nancy as she joined

them. "What is faith?"

"Faith is knowing something is real—

even when you cannot touch it,"

said Mr. Conductor.

"Just like a rainbow," said Nancy.

"Yes," said Mr. Conductor.

"Faith is knowing something is real—
even when you cannot see it."

"Like when the clouds covered
up the sun today," said Stevie.

"I couldn't see the sun,
but I knew it was there."

"You had faith,"
said Mr. Conductor.

"When you have faith,
you always feel as if
you stepped inside
the rainbow."

═ SELF-CONTROL DAY ═

"Tomorrow there will be surprises

for everyone," said Mr. Conductor.

"But today is self-control day."

He pointed to a pretty red box

on the ground outside his house.

"There is your surprise, Nancy."

He pointed to a pretty green box.

"There is your surprise, Stevie.

But you cannot open the surprises

until tomorrow.

That's why today is self-control day."

Stevie and Nancy picked flowers

in the meadow.

Then they came back and looked

at their boxes.

They ate dinner.

Then they came back and looked

at their boxes.

Finally Stevie said,

"I am going to sleep now.

That way tomorrow will come quickly."

Soon everyone in Agapeland

was asleep.

Nancy was tired.

But she could not sleep.

She stayed by her box.

I will make sure my box is safe,

she thought.

The red box shone in the moonlight.

I'll just shake the box once,

Nancy thought.

Nancy shook the box.

Back and forth.

Up and down.

It made a noise

and felt heavy.
The box was just too
interesting to put down.

I'll pull the ribbon a little,
she thought.
Then she remembered Mr. Conductor's
words.
"You cannot open the surprises until
tomorrow."

"Now I know what self-control is,"
she said out loud.
"It is doing what is right,
even when you don't want to."

Nancy put the box back down

on the ground.

She lay down beside it.

She said Mr. Conductor's words

over and over and over again.

Finally she fell asleep.

In the morning,

Mr. Conductor woke her.

"I am glad you had self-control, Nancy.

You may open your surprise now."

Nancy opened the pretty red box.

Twelve butterflies flew out.

They danced in the sunlight.

Then they rested on Nancy's arms.

"They are beautiful!" Nancy said.

"Thank you, Mr. Conductor."

"The butterflies thank you, Nancy,"

said Mr. Conductor.

"They were still forming

in their cocoons last night.

If you had let them out,

they would have died."

The butterflies flew around

and around and around Nancy.

They dipped their wings

as if to say, "Thank you."

One day a little breeze went

to see the Great South Wind.

"I want to be a great wind like you,"

said the little breeze.

"Will you teach me?"

"Yes," said the South Wind.

"But before you are a great wind,

you must learn to be a gentle breeze."

South Wind took the little breeze to

a garden in Agapeland.

"Blow here," said South Wind.

"Your breeze will cool off this garden.

But blow gently."   55

The little breeze looked around the
garden.

There was a big tree with yellow leaves.

The little breeze rushed over.

It *whooshed* around the tree.

The leaves tickled the little breeze.

"How quick I am!" it said.

The little breeze *whooshed* around
and around and around.

Faster and faster and faster.

Soon all the leaves fell off the tree.

They fell into the pond below.

"Oh, no!" said South Wind. "You are not being gentle. Tomorrow I will take you to see the Great North Wind. Maybe he can teach you to be a gentle breeze."

The next day South Wind took the little breeze to see North Wind.
Together they went to a beautiful meadow.
"Blow here, little breeze," said North Wind.

"Your breeze will cool off this meadow.
But blow gently."

There was a butterfly in the meadow.
"Let's play," it called.
Little breeze and the butterfly
danced and danced.
They danced around and around and
around.
Harder and harder and harder.
"How strong I am!" said little breeze.
But the butterfly grew dizzy.
It fell down to the ground.

The little breeze was sad.
"I am quick and strong," it said.
"But I don't know how to be gentle."

"It is good to be fast,"
said South Wind.
"But not too fast."

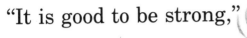

"It is good to be strong,"
said North Wind.
"But not too strong.
Let's try again."

The two great winds took the little
breeze to a house close by.
They told little breeze to look in the window.
A little baby lay there.
He was hot and sick.
And he was crying.

Louder and louder and louder.

"Blow here, little breeze," said the winds.

"Your breeze will cool the baby

and help him sleep.

But blow gently."

Instead of blowing faster and faster,

the little breeze blew slowly.

Instead of blowing harder and harder,

the little breeze blew softly.

Soon the baby stopped crying.

He closed his eyes and went to sleep.

The little breeze was very happy.

"Now you can be a great wind," said

North Wind.

"For now you know how to be gentle."

══ CAMPFIRE ══

Fireflies lit the night sky.

Stevie, Nancy, and Mr. Conductor

sat around a campfire with their friends.

Herbert the snail, Lamb, and Mr.

Squirrel were there.

A soft breeze blew through the trees.

Everyone was singing the
Music Machine songs.
Songs of love, patience, and joy.
Songs of goodness, faith, and gentleness.
Songs of kindness and self-control.
All the lessons Stevie and Nancy
had learned in Agapeland.

Stevie and Nancy grew very tired.
They lay down in a bed of clover
near the machine.
"We have learned many wonderful
things," said Nancy.

"And you know what?" Stevie said.

"I feel different inside."

"Me, too," said Nancy.

"It feels good to do what

is right," said Stevie.

"It feels like peace."

"The fruit of the Spirit is love, joy, peace,

patience, kindness, goodness,

faithfulness, gentleness and self-control."

Galatians 5: 22